# The Power of

# Perseverance

# SHERI SIMMONS & SHAVONA
# WARMINGTON

ISBN: 978-0-9853199-8-4

The Power of Perseverance
Written by Sheri Simons & Shavona Warmington
Copyright © 2020 by Sheri Simmons

## Acknowledgments

I truly thank God that I don't look like what I been through! This is my first anthology that I put together. I am so amazed at the talent of my friend and sister Shavona. Thank you for trusting me with your work! Now let's show the world what we are made of. To my family, I thank you for everything. I am grateful to have you all in my life. To my friends, thank you guys for being my support system. To anyone I forgot, blame my mind not my heart. I thank everyone who has ever purchased a book, said kind word or just helped me along my journey. You are greatly appreciated.

Sheri Simmons

# The Power of Perseverance

# 360°

Shavona Warmington

First and foremost, Alhamduillah!!! None of what I went through was in vain, it has made me stronger in the end.

Special thanks to my children for being the biggest reason for me holding on and fighting for better...for them and myself. To my mother for learning the many faces of abuse and survival while helping me get it together. To my stronger half, Supreme for being my coach when I fell off my game and keeping me super focused while loving all my broken pieces. There are truly blessings in life's lessons.

# The Power of Perseverance

hen I think of the journey I have been on dealing with all the trials I have faced and then I look at where I am TODAY, I can definitely say there really is not enough minutes in my life to truly explain how I did it. There are still countless times I look back and ask myself; 'how?'. I still cannot get a solid answer. To the mere mortal mind, overcoming obstacles tends to instill a fear in each of us that can end up leaving u paralyzed emotionally, physically, and mentally.

We may be stuck with what mentally scared us. We may be stuck with what seems to be one of two viable options. One is giving up on moving forward due to fear of the unknown and just retreating back to familiar grounds regardless of how toxic the soil. The other option is to be a prisoner of one's own thoughts — doubt that one may actually be able to succeed — and remain stagnant. Neither of these two options will help any of us if our ultimate goal is to progress and advance to the next level of greatness.

We have all been generationally conditioned to accept defeat as an immediate response when faced with opposition. We tend to always see the options readily made accessible, despite them not being the only options. Nobody tends to look up. We have learned to carry our pain and allow it to weigh us down just that much that "up" never becomes a thought.

My journey of my pain began in my high school years. My teenage years were a whirlwind. I do not remember spending much time enjoying them. I was working while every one of my classmates were caught up socializing and being teens. I was too busy making money. When I entered high school, I was inducted into the scholar's society.

Unfortunately, I was not able to stay focused, so I was dropped from that and fell amongst the general population of my high school's student body.

At that time, I was battling the beginning of what is now the immigration chaos occurring currently. My father was already deported but the biggest fear was losing my mother. I was working evening and weekends at the local hair salon washing and braiding the clients' hair. I knew how to do the full head weaves, but I decided to build my own clientele base instead of paying for a booth rental. I also had my own line of cosmetic and ethnic skin and hair care products that I started making so I was not about to go through hoops trying to keep my earnings. I understood that if anything happened to my mother I would be on my own. Of course, I had relatives, but I learned at a very early age that no matter how much family a person has, when tragedy strikes you are as alone as a huge stone amongst grains of desert sand.

I started preparing myself for whatever may come. The last thing a 16-year-old should have to worry about was losing her parents due to a country's leaders deciding immigrants were toxic to their growth. I should have been focused on looking beautiful at prom and counting down to graduation. I was on the road to growing way too fast. I was walking the road paved for adults, but my teenage mind was engulfed in the fast money and the freedom that came with it. I had good grades and never missed any classes, so no one really had to worry about me. I also did not look my age so when I needed to get things done, I did not have to answer any major questions.

I was pregnant my senior year of high school and learned the reality of life, death and losses the hard way. As happy as I was and as confused as I was, I had to come to terms with Heaven needing my son more than I did. I learned to be cold from that day as I was not ready to nor could I understand why. I learned what depression was just as early.

I was in a dark place and the father was hard since he was "playing the field" and nobody else knew or needed to know outside of our disappointed parents. I let myself get consumed by work once again, except I found a different line of income and much faster. I started working in the night clubs and used this environment as a distraction from what I was going through.

Nobody knew my age, they only seen a mature body. They also knew I was serious about my money. Being the new girl, I prepared myself for the competition. I also knew that the patrons would try and test the waters. I learned very fast I was in the minority in this game because I did not do "dates", I only danced. I made a name for myself very fast being that I worked alone, traveled alone, kept my tips and paid my tip ins way ahead of time. I got invited to do private parties, but I was very selective. I found working the strip clubs to be an escape since my stage name and my alter ego drowned out my real-life pain.

I, of course, faced the reality every day I went to school or walked the streets. My line of work paid for college, so I had no complaints, I had a car and regular day job as well. I was doing good. I graduated high school a year early so nothing halted my studies. At least until the moment I met the person that did not change my life for the better but for the worst.

I met my daughter's father while shopping for groceries. He walked up to me and asked me for my number and at first, I was not going to give it to him but the way he approached me made me give him a shot. I was single at the time and working while being the typical college student. We spoke over the phone mostly because I was living my life working and going to school. I did not know his past because trust me I would not have given him the time of day. He went away for a while due to parole violation and the ignorant me (and I say ignorant because I did not know what he had done prior to meeting me) stayed by his side. When he came home, I let myself be blinded by what I thought was love.

I did not realize he was conditioning me for what would have been the worst 7 years of my life. The person that I thought loved me started to control me. He wanted to know where I was at all times. He found ways to keep me away from my friends and family. He monitored my funds and manipulated my life in every way he could. He was released on parole so he would call me to pick him up so he could be home before curfew however that ended up being a free ride for his friends. He started degrading me publicly. I started to lose myself with each verbal attack. I allowed myself to believe all of what he seen me as.

In 2012, on the 5th of January I found that he was cheating, and I got myself dressed and walked out. He ran from behind and knocked me unconscious. When I came to, I was told I was pregnant by the nurses at Peninsula Hospital which was in Far Rockaway Queens, NY. I was pregnant for my abuser. I endured a stressful and abusive pregnancy but managed to find refuge back at my mother's house in time to really rest and prepare for delivery.

I was able to bring my daughter home to a safe place. I was wrong. My abuser found ways to harass me there. My abuser used ACS to track my whereabouts and the family court did not make it any better. I was not going to throw the towel in though.

The last battle really begun in 2017. My abuser threatened to kill my children and me after learning I was engaged. I had to pick up and leave my home, quit my job and go into protective housing. I could have easily given up then. I was tired. I was overwhelmed. The courts did not seem to be listening. I was at the bottom. I lost friends and family turned away to avoid any involvement with the drama. This all seemed dismal until I had a real long talk with myself and the first question, I asked myself was "Is this going to be it?" I dried my tears and kept repeating that question over and over in my head. I looked over at my daughters asleep and a voice inside said "It's not over yet!" I started reaching out to lawyers and looking into all the laws that were set to protect people in my position. I found a lawyer that agreed to help me with the false ACS claims and for no charge. I spoke to my professors and the president of the college I attended, and they found a way to help me finish my last few classes online so I would not be delayed for graduation. I was given an externship site that worked with my situation as well. When I reached out to my church and told them what was going on, they blessed me to be able to give my girls the best holidays despite the situation.

The minute I stopped waking with my head down and looked UP, everything started to go in a different direction. The courts granted me full, sole and physical custody of my daughter while granting only visitation to the father. I was eventually hired for a city job and took myself and my daughters out of the shelter. I was able to pick up my cap and gown and the day I walked graduation was one of the proudest days as well as the most emotional day.

All the turmoil I went through poured out in emotional tears as my daughters saw me collect OUR degree. Pain from my teenage years all the way through to present day still run from my face from time to time but I sit and look at what I have accomplished by holding my head UP and pushing forward. A college graduate. A medical professional as well as now being in Social Services. A Domestic Violence Advocate. An author. A mentor. Pain was designed to handicap us. That does not mean that we have to allow it to.

I chose to stop carrying my pain and to build off it. I used it to become much greater than what others expected me to be. I found the ME that existed before I allowed myself to be broken and I rebuilt and revamped until I was renewed, and my mind was reloaded. I told myself I would never allow that to happen again as long as I kept true to myself and understood that anything that would cost me ME was costing me way too much. Resilience makes way to greatness with the push of perseverance!

# Motherless Child

## SHERI SIMMONS

Sheri Simmons & Shavona Warmington

# Chapter One

My name is Janell Thompson. When I was 16, discovered my mom was an excessive gambler. I didn't know the full details of what gambling was, but I knew her actions were causing a lot of problems. Who wants to be evicted or sit in the dark of their apartment? It happened to me quite a few times and my mom made it seem like it was nothing. As if this was a normal part of life.

Gambling is an addiction and just like any addict they just don't care about anything but when they are gonna get their next "fix". At first, the fix for my mom was playing numbers. Then she moved on to casinos. She would go nearly every weekend when I was a teen. All of this activity took a toll on not just my mom, but me and my siblings. I spent countless nights worrying about where and when my mom was coming home. Often times felt like I was the parent and she was the child.

When your addicted to something, you want to have it by any means necessary. So, if it means, lying, cheating and stealing so be it. I had no idea that when my mom was sending me to her friends to ask for money that she was using it to gamble. She didn't say it was for that. She would say things like "my kids need shoes" or whatever else she could think of. But all I could think of was how much of a hypocrite she was. She used to always get on me and my siblings about lying but yet she lied all the time to get what she wanted. My young heart was completely conflicted on what to believe. Do you lie to people to get what you want, or do you work hard to get what you want?

My mom was the Devil on my shoulder and my grandmother was the Angel. My grandmother always had something good or positive to say while my mom gave me bad things to do. My grandma taught me the power of hard work and maintaining my integrity. My mom taught me that money ruled the world and I needed to get it how I get it.

School was my solace from the pain I felt at home. I knew once I got home that everything would be on me to do. To get everyone ready for school, make sure everyone ate and did their homework. But as my siblings and I got older it became a huge problem. They didn't want to listen, and I got tired of talking. I quickly ended up depressed and searched desperately for a way out. Anything to get me away from home and my siblings was where I wanted to be. It's not healthy for children to be put in adult situations and expected to act accordingly. I felt like my mom expected things to go on as if she was home. And if anything was wrong or out of order, I felt her wrath. Often times I got yelled at for someone not doing their homework or someone not listening in school. It was just so much pressure for me to play mom and be who I was at the same time. I didn't even know who I was. I never had time to discover anything. I was suffocating and needed space. As days turned into months, months into years, I grew miserable. Misery turned into depression. I didn't know whether I was coming or going. The burden of taking care of myself and them was literally killing me. There was so much pain and despair inside of me. But I had to keep a smile on my face. I couldn't dare speak about the torture that I was enduring at home. I couldn't let anyone know that my mother had mentally and emotionally checked out of her role. That she was hardly home, and I was the one keeping everything and everyone together.

To the world, my mom was perfect. She took well care of me and gave me what I wanted. I heard people say I was lucky to be able to go to Girl Scouts, Dance Class and all these activities. However, I beg to differ. My needs as a kid were not being met at all. I felt tortured and miserable. I wasn't asked to attend any of these things. She placed me in them to help my socialization skills. Little did she know I was sinking into depression. Of course, depression didn't have a name like it does today. There was no mental health awareness like there is today.

Because of the fact that I was depressed, my personality changed. I became quieter and more withdrawn. My mom thought I was anti-social because I refused to talk or be around people. To this day she says that I am anti-social. That's not true. Because of her, I am socially selective. I don't dwell in toxicity period! I don't care who it comes from!

*Exodus 20:12 says "Honor your father and mother, so that you may live long in the land the Lord, your God is giving you."* I struggled with this scripture from the first time I heard it and even now. Honor the people who both abandoned me at a young age. My father left when I was six years old. No explanation just walked right out the door. They never taught me how to be a productive, positive person? They created all this darkness and despair inside of me? Honor them for what purpose? I didn't ask to be born and yet they brought me into their lives. Just to mess up my life before it even truly began.

## Chapter Two

I was raised in the Bronx until the age of six. We moved to Manhattan and my Daddy left me at the same time. What a traumatic day it was. All I remember was him walking away and not turning back as I cried. I was blessed with six years with him; most kids never have seen their fathers. That's the sad but accurate truth. I had no clue why my daddy left me at the tender of six. It hurt but it was a hurt that I was quickly able to get over. Kids adjust but the trauma remains, I know this now.

After my father left, my mother moved my sister, and I, to the east side of Harlem aka Spanish Harlem. I was enjoying my life, until my mom brought home a baby boy. I always wanted a brother. Now that I had one, I had no idea he would be my responsibility. I learned early on how to make formula, change diapers, burp and hold a baby. My childhood was gone because I spent all my time (when not in school) with my siblings.

Things became worse when my mother brought home yet another baby two years later. After my mom brought her home, she gave me a key and gave me instructions on what to do. I had to make sure everyone got to school or daycare, pick everyone up and have things in order by the time my mom came back. Some days, she wouldn't return until late night. My mom worked from six am to two pm. However, she was rarely home when we came from school. In the beginning it didn't really matter but as I got older it put a strain on my teenage social life. Ultimately, I didn't get to experience anything most teenagers did.

Playing the role of mommy to children that were not mine was grueling and unbearable. At eight years old, I was left alone to watch a newborn. I dropped my sister once, because the crib bar was not lowered. I was trying to lower the bar and hold the baby, but she fell. I panicked as I picked up the crying baby. Her complexion changed from a high-yellow color to a reddish-pink. I laid her down on the bed, because I didn't know what else to do. Thankfully, thirty minutes later, my mom came. She didn't hit me, because she knew it was her fault, but she did give me a good tongue-lashing, using the words "stupid" and "crazy". Her words hurt more than the physical beatings. Whoever came up with the phrase, "Sticks and stones may break my bones, but words will never hurt me, is a liar! Words do hurt and back then, I was always the victim of my mom's awful words. My self-esteem was so low for a long time. I would not

speak up for myself or even look people in
their eyes.

I would get in trouble for any little thing
they did, such as not doing their homework
and coming in late. I couldn't go anywhere
without them. One time, I was invited to a
sleepover; my mom said I could go, but I had
to take my siblings with me. There was no way
I was taking them to hang out with my friends.
I was trapped in the house on weekends. I was
determined to make it my way out of hell. The
older we got, the more my mom stayed away.
The more I focused on getting my high school
diploma, the crazier things became in my life.

## Chapter Three

Around the age of twelve, I felt like I was losing my sanity. I had no peace of mind and nowhere to escape my daily problems. I sank into a deep dark depression. I became withdrawn and kept to myself. People started classifying me as shy and quiet, which is not true at all. I became so overwhelmed. This was the age where I had my first suicidal thought and attempt.

A twelve-year-old girl should be out with her friends, being able to explore the world with boundaries and rules; not caged in a house watching after three kids. If I wanted to go somewhere, I had to take them with me. It became a bit too much, so I began to have thoughts of dying. If I died, what would my mom do then? She would have no choice, but to be responsible for these children she created.

No one was responsible for me, and yet I had the responsibility of three children.

I'd had enough and one day, I decided to make my suicidal thoughts come true. Coming home from school one day, I grabbed the first knife I could find and locked myself in the bathroom. I began rubbing it across my wrist. I looked at it and realized that it was a butter knife; it wouldn't cause me much damage if I did slit my wrist. However, it would land me in the hospital, which would get me out of the hell I was in. Just when I had the courage to start cutting, there was a knock on the door. I put the knife down and opened it, but no one was there. I returned the knife, went in my room and laid down. "Something has to give!" I shouted. I looked across the room and noticed a writing pad. It was black and spiral bounded at the top. I had this for a while and never had any real use for it until today. One of my mother's friends had given it to me. I picked up a pen and let the words flow on the paper.

*Dear Diary*

*Why do I have to live this life? I am 12 years old and I feel like I'm 30. I should be having fun with my friends and going places, but I can't, because I have to bring my siblings everywhere, I go. Sometimes I just want to run away, but I don't know where to go. The only time I get to have freedom and peace is in school. I can't wait 'til I can get out of here and leave all this behind.*

*I just attempted to slit my wrist, but I couldn't do it. All these thoughts and emotions were running through my head. I can't live like this anymore. Starting today, I will focus on school, which I feel is my ticket out of here.*

After my first entry that night, I was hooked on journal writing. It was my way to release my pain without causing harm to myself or anyone else. After I had filled up the journal, I asked my mother's friend where he'd gotten it. He said that he made them at work and if I wanted more, he would make me some. He came back with a box full of journals; I was so grateful that I would be able to continue writing. Writing helped me to stay focused on my goal of graduating high school and I became a new person.

## *Chapter Four*

I graduated high school at 17 years old turning 18 within the next month. I had been accepted to a community college and a university in Atlanta. Georgia for me meant freedom. I wanted to be on my own, far away from my family. I wanted so badly to go Atlanta, but my mother killed my dream. There was a one-hundred-dollar deposit needed to hold my seat and my mother said she didn't have it, so I couldn't go. I went to community college with no set goals in mind. I also left my mom's house. I'd done everything she'd ever asked me to do. My siblings were now sixteen, twelve, and ten; I felt I didn't owe my mother anything. She said to me that now that I had graduated and turned 18, I was cut off. I didn't know what that meant. Seeing that I was about to start college and didn't have a job, I just figured she was going to help me out. But no, I was literally on my own. I figured if I was going to be on my own, I might as well be away from her. And so, I left the home that caused me so much misery in my childhood. I was excited and scared at the same time. I had no idea what was out there in the world, but I was ready to face whatever was out there.

I moved in with my best friend, Venessa and her family. They welcomed me with open arms. I was no longer confined to being in the house; I was eighteen and free as a bird, or so I thought. Since my childhood was taken away, I ran around free as a horse with my hair blowing in the breeze. Because of the fact growing up there were no rules, curfews or any authority figures, I struggled with listening to Venessa's mom. She gave me a curfew which I violated so many times. She wanted me to wash dishes and do laundry for everyone in the house. I was very rebellious towards her. It was really bad for me because I was 18 and had no clue how to wash dishes, do laundry or cook. I didn't know how to do these things because all I had to do was go to school and watch my siblings. We ate a lot of take out as kids, so I never learned to use a stove or oven. My mom washed the clothing every Sunday.

I quickly realized that I didn't know crap about being an adult. And even though it was a constant fight with Venessa's mom she always included me in everything she did with her own children. It was strange at first being part of a family that ate dinner and watched tv together. But I quickly got used to it. I suddenly realized if I wanted to survive in the world as an adult, I needed to adapt to whatever situation I was placed in. People say that is called survival mode. If adjusting and adapting is survival mode, then I have been in that mode most of my life.

********************************************

The Girl Scout program that I was in was inside of a church. When I turned 16 years old, I decided I wanted to be baptized. I didn't really understand what was going on or what it was about. I knew that I wanted to belong to a family and church to me had people in it that I considered family. So, I continued going to church every Sunday learning as much as I could about God. But of course, I got sidetracked when I met a young man one day. The man I met turned out to be one of the worst men I ever had. I hated myself, during and after my relationship with him. He completely flipped my world upside down

The first year of our relationship was okay, just minor fights and arguments. Who doesn't have those? We were making moves as two responsible adults. I was finally away from everyone and in my own apartment. I also got a job as a personal care aide. For me, life wasn't perfect, but I was fine. Every time I get to be comfortable, something happened to knock me back down to the ground. A couple of days before Christmas, I discovered that I was pregnant.

## Chapter Five

I was not happy knowing I was pregnant. It just wasn't what I wanted. But he was thrilled and started calling everybody. For the sake of peace in the house I pretended to be excited even though I wasn't. It wasn't long before my heart was shattered into many pieces.

After an argument one day, I was told that I wasn't wanted nor was the baby. My brain couldn't comprehend what was being said to me. All I knew was that I had a decision to make and I had to make it fast. I didn't even know how many weeks I was or where to go for prenatal care. The stress of making decisions that affected someone else made me so sick. After four agonizing days I decided to terminate my pregnancy.

The day I went to terminate the pregnancy, I wasn't alone. I wish I was though. I definitely didn't need to be called a murderer every five minutes. It was too much for me to bear so I asked him to remove himself which he did. Now I was left alone to continue with what I started.

After I filled out a stack of paperwork, I was given a sonogram to determine the age of the fetus. When I was told I was seven weeks, I nearly passed out. The technician asked me if I wanted to complete the process and I nodded yes. I was not allowed to see the baby on the screen, because she had the screen turned away from me. After the sonogram, I was sent back out to the waiting room. I was alone and seeing all the other women around me, made me feel worse than what I was already feeling.

I just wanted to get it over with. Knowing that she would be no help, I called my mother. I asked her to come to me. In all honesty, I just wanted someone to tell me not to go through with the procedure. She told me she was busy and couldn't come and it hurt like hell. When they called my name, I was scared. I entered the room, scared to death, heartbroken and alone.

When I woke up, I had to look around several times. I was in the most horrible pain. When I was escorted to the recovery room, I ended up vomiting all over myself. I felt horrible; I just wanted to curl up like a ball and die.

After an hour-long wait in the recovery room, I took a cab to Venessa's house. I just wanted to lie my weak body down. I cried my eyes out all night and just like the loyal friend that she is, she cried right along with me. I was too through with Tony. Or so I thought.

I thought I was over Tony. To be honest, I don't know why I went back. I realized later on that people allow others to have control over them. For another whole year, I suffered in silence. The abuse got worse each day. I lived with hearing how stupid I was, that no one wanted me, how much of a "bitch", and" hoe" I was. I had tables, chairs, bikes, whatever was in arm's reach thrown at me. He even went as low as to raping me. I felt so degraded after that night, yet still, I stayed. Eventually the stress of staying caused me to leave. I was so stressed that I lost my hair and tremendous amount of weight. I felt like at any given moment I was going to die. So, I decided to go back where I knew I was loved.

I called Venessa to help me pack all my belongings. She helped me to pack all of my stuff and get out of there before he came back. Once again, I ended up staying in Venessa's house. I was always welcomed back there, no matter what I was going through.

It seemed that I had decided to move on and not look back. I can freely admit with no problem that I was young and dumb. Not knowing anything about being in love and what love is supposed to be. At first, I blamed myself for not knowing any better. I realized, as I got older that my father created a complex in me. The first man in my life abandoned me. I never knew how love from a man was supposed to feel like, so I settled. This would not be the last time I saw myself in a domestic violence situation.

When he discovered that I had left, he kept calling me. I refused to answer his calls. As Christmas time approached, I started to miss him, and loneliness started to settle in. Against my better judgment, I went to go spend Christmas Day with him and his nephew, who happened to be my godson. I nearly paid for my mistake with my life.

Everything was going ok until I decided that I was ready to leave. As I gathered up my belongings and put on my coat he headed to the door. I didn't pay him much mind until I was ready to leave. As I approached the door, he asked me where I was going. I explained that I was tired and wanted to go home. He wasn't having that as an answer. He insisted that I was going to my new boyfriend's house. I was not about to argue with him and asked him to move from the door. And that's when all hell broke loose. He knocked me down on

The Power of Perseverance

the floor and pulled out a big knife. I instantly
backed up and looked for a way out. But of
course, there wasn't one. He had locked the
door that he was standing at. There was a
window that I could go through, but I knew
the path was a dead end. I had tried to escape
his many physical episodes before that way.
The closer he got to me, the more I knew I was
going to die. I was terrified and shaking very
badly as he stood over me and said "If I can't
have you. No One else can. When I felt the first
blow, I looked down at my arm and saw blood.
I screamed bloody murder. To shut me up he
delivered blow after blow, after blow to my
108-pound body. There were moments where I
blacked out and he would shake me violently
to wake me up. I know what a punching bag
feel like. The attack felt like it went on for
hours. And just like that he carried me outside,
hailed a cab and told the driver where I was

53

going. The driver saw that I was disoriented and asked me did I want to go to the police station. I said no. I just wanted to go to sleep.

At the end of the day, I had a deep wound on my arm, and broken ribs on my left side. I was officially done before I even knew it. God has a way of forcing us to move out of certain situations. I didn't want to move, but God shook me up to make moves. I am thankful to be alive. I am also thankful to have gone through this experience—no regrets at all, but a whole lot of lessons learned. Now I was back at square one. I lost everything I had on my own messing with him. I decided I needed to get my life back on track. So, I enrolled in school again.

# Chapter Six

This time when I enrolled in school, I had to pay to attend. The plight of wanting to do better but not having the means really bothered me. I was back at Venessa's house. I didn't want her parents or anyone else to know the trouble that I had been in so I decided to get a job that would make me some quick fast cash. I didn't want to be a dancer but hey the pay was sweet, and the hours were flexible.

Being a full-time student and dancing at night was exhausting. I didn't get much sleep at all, but I was making a load of money. For once in my life, I was happy. I moved out on my own and even got a car. I was living life the way I wanted and not for anyone else. However, as they say, all things come to an end. After three months of dancing, my life took a turn for the worse. The unthinkable happened to me and I just couldn't handle my emotions. I didn't know what to do or who to turn to.

The day my best friend died, I died a mental and emotional death. I couldn't get out of my bed, nor did I enjoy any of the things I used to do. My grandmother was like a mother to me since my own mother left me to survive on my own. She didn't teach me a damn thing about life. I knew the day would come when God would take my grandmother, but I wasn't prepared for it. I wasn't prepared for anything that life brought to me.

When I was a teenager, my grandmother moved to Atlanta. I wanted to go with her, but my mom declined. When I got accepted into a university in Atlanta, my mom declined that too. She knew how close I was with my grandmother. I knew my mom was a hater; I was just too through with my mother. It bothered me because I just couldn't understand why she hated me.

The day of my grandmother's funeral, I was sick to my stomach. I did not want to see my grandmother lying in a casket. I was still in a state of shock. I knew that I had to be strong to help my aunt and uncle get through this ordeal.

My grandmother died alone in a nursing home. I will forever live with the fact that I wasn't there. The last time I saw her was New Year Day. We brought the New Year together. I would have taken the trip if I had known I would never see her again

After the funeral, my mom ended up leaving my brother, and taking my two sisters' home. It was good-bye and good riddance, as far as I was concerned! No one cared that she had left. No one that is, except my brother. For the first time in my life, I saw my little brother have an emotional breakdown. He couldn't understand for the life of him why she had left him stranded there. All I could do was shake my head and tell him, "I told you your day would come" and walk away. I told my brother for years how our mom treated me, and he always justified her behavior. Telling me "You know how she is," or "Just ignore her" He wanted me to ignore her, but he couldn't at the moment. He literally drank himself sick. I couldn't sleep with the sound of him vomiting his guts out.

My grandmother was gone, so there were no ties to my mom. I didn't speak to my mom unless my grandmother told me to throughout my life, my grandma was always the peacemaker between my mom and me. Now I was all by myself literally.

While everyone else headed back to
New York, I stayed in Atlanta to figure out
what I was going to do with my life. I was on
summer break from school, so I had two and a
half months to get myself together. Life as I
knew it was over. Yeah, I had started school
and was making money, but I'd lost my
biggest support system. Life was so unfair.

During my stay in Atlanta, I
stayed in my grandmother's house. It felt so
weird being in her house without her. For the
first couple of days there, I had weird dreams
where she would come back and speak to me.

*"Why are you moping around?"* she said,
*"When are you gonna get married?"*

I laughed and knew then that she had
never left me. I could still talk to her whenever
I wanted to. After days of being in the house, I
decided to head out and explore. With no

destination in mind, I got in my car and drove. I wanted to go to the beach. I couldn't swim, but I loved to walk the boardwalk of Atlantic City. I checked the map and lo and behold, I found Tybee Island, Georgia. Tybee Island was a good three-hour drive from where my grandmother stayed. I had nothing but time, so I headed out to clear my head. With "Rich Girl" by Eve and Gwen Stefani blasting, I drove to take in the sights.

## Chapter seven

I loved shopping; it filled a huge void that I had. The void of feeling unloved, the void of having such low self-esteem. I was five foot two and wore glasses. I was one hundred and twenty pounds. Dealing with assholes and a momma who called me stupid and ugly, it hurt so much. So, I shopped to make myself feel better about myself. It worked the same way people ate to feel better. It doesn't make sense from the outside looking in, but what works for me is for me. Fortunately for me Tybee Island had tons of retail shops for me to visit

I felt my cell phone vibrating and instantly got annoyed. I wasn't looking to speak to anyone. I was in my own zone. I looked at the caller ID and smiled.

"Yes," I answered with a smile.

"I haven't seen you in a week. Where you disappear to?" Quincy asked me with concern in his voice.

"Thanks for being concerned. I am okay. Just needed a break," I answered nonchalantly.

I had butterflies in my stomach. Quincy and I went on a few dates and instantly hit it off. However, I learned from my past mistakes and didn't want to make them again. Plus, I met him in a club. So, I took my time and got to know this beautiful man that made me feel like a queen. He was chocolate colored, tall and had a dark Caesar. He was so thoughtful and caring, I felt like I was dreaming. I had fallen for the Prince Charming act before and remembered where that'd gotten me. I was happy with the way things were. I loved being single and free, but able to have male company when I wanted it.

"Are you sure everything is okay?" he questioned me.

I was a bad liar. I didn't have a quick enough comeback.

"You can tell me," he insisted.

Sighing softly, I replied, "I am in Atlanta right now. My grandmother passed away."

"I'm so sorry to hear that. Is there anything I can do? Anything that you need?" he sincerely asked me.

I didn't know what to say or do, so I said nothing.

"Hey baby, you still there?" he asked me.

"Yes, I'm still here. I don't know what to say right now," I admitted to him.

"You don't have to be shy or pretend with me," he assured me.

"That's nice to know," I said, smiling.

"When are you coming back to New York?"

"I don't know, honestly. I haven't had the chance to grieve yet," I said sadly.

"Would you like some company?" he asked.

I was longing to be held and just cry my eyes out to someone. I didn't cry over my grandmother's death at all. I didn't shed a tear over the nasty argument I had with my mother. She revealed to me that everything she'd done for me; she didn't want to do. I knew that, but to hear her finally say it, felt like someone stabbed me in my heart. From that day, I didn't speak to my mother.

Against my better judgment, I asked Quincy to join me in Atlanta. He said he would be taking the next flight out. Putting my phone away, I smiled as I thought of having fun with Quincy. He seemed like such a gentleman, but all that glittered wasn't gold.

## Chapter Eight

When Quincy arrived at the airport; I was there to pick him up. I wasn't comfortable taking him to my grandmother's house, so he suggested a week's stay at a hotel. I agreed. I had no idea he meant a five-star hotel. I knew I was someplace luxurious upon driving up to the entrance. We were at the Ritz Carlton. I was in awe at how spacious the place was. For a moment, I started to feel ashamed of myself. I was supposed to be grieving the loss of my grandma, not meeting up with a crush. However, when Quincy got out of the car and opened my door, extending his hand, all of my thoughts went out of the window.

"Don't be scared, baby. I don't bite… Unless you want me to," Quincy said, smiling at me with his perfectly white teeth.

*The Power of Perseverance*

My panties instantly moistened. *He can definitely get it,* I thought as I smiled back. He took my hand and led me into the hotel. I felt so special, but I was a bit conflicted. Every time I allow myself to catch feelings for a man, I got more than my feelings hurt. I got my self-esteem, body, and pride hurt. I kept trying to tell myself that he was different, but my mind was saying, *Yeah right!* While Quincy went to pay for the room, I stood off to the side. *What the hell I am doing with this man?* I thought. I suddenly wanted to go home, back to my comfort zone. I needed some hardcore advice, before I ended up doing something stupid. I yanked out my cell phone and called Venessa.

"Hey," I said, sadly.

"What happened now?" she sighed.

"Well, you remember Quincy?" I sighed.

"Yeah, that guy who kept calling you non-stop and buying you whatever you wanted. Does he have a younger brother?" she laughed.

"This is not the time to joke!" I said, seriously.

"Okay…What's going on between y'all?" she asked, mocking my serious tone.

"Well, he came down here to keep me company. Right now, we are at the nice ass hotel. I want to come home. Tell me to come home!" I demanded.

"Come home then. It's boring without you," she said nonchalantly.

"That's it? That's all you have to say?" I said in despair.

"Get that fine man before someone else gets him. That's all I have to say."

I shook my head. Quincy was heading my way. "Thanks for nothing," I whispered as I ended the call.

"You ready, baby?" he asked me as he scooped me into his arms.

I smiled and put my game face on. "As ready as I'll ever be." He let go of the embrace and took my hand, leading me up to our room.

When we got up to the room, I gasped. It looked like a honeymoon suite. In front of me was a huge, king size bed, with rose petals in it. Nearby lay a bottle of champagne and chocolate-covered strawberries. I let go of his hand and looked around. There was a heart-shaped Jacuzzi that looked so inviting. We had a refrigerator and a complete dining room area. I looked back at Quincy and felt the tears flowing down my eyes. "Why?" I asked him.

"Why what?" he asked me, confused.

"Why are you being so nice to me?" I questioned him.

"I like you a lot. I would like to get to know more of you. You are a very bright and beautiful young woman. Why wouldn't I treat you like the queen you are?"

"I can't," I said, trying to brush past him and open the door.

"I don't understand what I did wrong," he said, side eyeing me.

I knew I looked and sounded stupid, but I didn't care. I wasn't about to fall for the lies of a man again. I lost my baby and almost my life over a man.

"I don't want to be hurt again. My heart can't take it," I sobbed as I collapsed into his arms.

He held me and said the infamous line I always heard, "I'm not here for that."

I heard him and should have left the room. Instead, I trusted and believed that he was here, because he had genuine feelings for me. For the past three months, he had been around me every day, making sure I wanted for nothing.

"I just don't know what to do anymore. My grandmother is gone, and I may have to leave school," I sighed.

"That's not happening," he said sternly. "What you need to do is be my woman and let me take care of you. You won't ever want for anything again."

"Seriously?" I stared in his eyes to see if I could see how serious he was.

He didn't respond. Instead, he picked me up and kissed my lips tenderly. I swear I almost melted; I felt so weak.

"Mmm," I moaned as I kissed him back.

He held my five-foot two frames high up from the floor. He stood six foot two. I couldn't take anymore. I tried to wiggle out of his arms.

"Where you think you going?" he asked me as he moved toward the bed.

I wiggled harder. I wasn't ready to make the next step with him. Despite all the time that we had spent together, we had never had sex. It was strange to me, but I felt it was best in order for me to think with a clear head. He laid me down and crawled on top of me. I could feel him rubbing up against me. *No! No! No!* I screamed in my head. However, my mouth said,

"Yes! Yes! Yes!"

I laid still as Quincy removed my clothes and kissed my stomach. I shuddered as he kissed me on my neck. I was growing anxious to feel him inside me; the more he teased me with his tongue. I wiggled my body underneath Quincy once again. He let me up and I ducked into the bathroom.

"What the hell is going on with me?" I asked myself aloud.

I turned the water on and splashed some on my face. Looking in the mirror, I sighed.

"What does he see that I don't?" I whispered.

I found myself questioning whether he was telling me the truth about how he felt.

Shaking my head, I walked back into the bedroom.

When I walked into the room, Quincy's mouth dropped open. His face expression turned me on. I strutted over to him; He didn't say anything as I continued walk towards him. "It is so on," he said to me.

As soon as I was close enough, he grabbed me and threw me down on the bed while I looked up at him in shock. My facial expression only turned him on more. He kissed me and my mind went into a place of complete ecstasy.

*******************************

"I need to talk to you about some things," I said, changing the subject. My demeanor had completely changed. He knew I was about to bring up some bull.

"I'm listening," he said, sitting up to give me his undivided attention.

"Can we take a shower and change the sheets first please?" I said, as I got up off the bed.

"You going to let me love you some more?" he asked, heading to the bathroom.

I followed him. "Whatever you say."

When we finally made it to bed, we were exhausted.

"So, what did you need to talk to me about?" Quincy asked.

I snuggled up under him. "I truly appreciate you."

He could feel a "but" coming. He stared into my brown eyes, trying to read mine. He saw hurt and despair in my facial expression. I took a deep breath and continued. "I can't help feeling incomplete." I buried my face into his chest. "I don't have a family. My grandmother was the closest person to me and now she's gone," I sobbed.

Quincy took me into his arms. "Don't worry Baby Girl. I got you."

I snuggled up in his arms and drifted off to sleep. The last words he spoke to me kept ringing in my ears. "Don't worry Baby Girl. I got you."

In that moment I should have left, but I didn't. I had a habit of staying in places and situations that I didn't belong. So many red flags popped up before this morning. I couldn't see them because my glasses were rose colored. By the time my vision became clear, it became too late.

# The Power of Perseverance

## *Chapter Nine*

The weekend Quincy and I spent in Atlanta was simply amazing. When he approached me over dinner with an 18K rose gold ring with a pink diamond center stone, I cried. He looked at me and picked my head up.

"Will you marry me?" he asked, getting down on one knee.

I started bawling and shaking at the same time. I couldn't believe what was happening right now.

"You gonna leave me down here?" he asked me impatiently.

"No," I whispered, looking into his eyes

"Is that your answer to my proposal?" he asked, staring at me intently.

I screamed in my head. He was waiting for an answer and I didn't have one. I was not in love, but I was getting there.

"Yes," I replied with tears in my eyes. He placed the ring on my finger and picked me up. I felt so safe and secure in his arms. Little did I know, this would be the last time I felt secure in his presence.

Before we headed home to New York, we were married. I was now Mrs. Janell Richardson. I was the happiest girl in the world until the day I was smacked so hard, I saw stars. According to my new husband, I had my eyes on some guy too long. That wasn't the case; I had my eye on a purse in the store window. The man just happened to be in plain view. As soon as his hand hit my face, I went off. He pushed me away. I came back after him and he slammed me against the wall so hard, I fell to the ground.

"Don't you ever disrespect me again!" he spat as he stared down at me.

I got up and ran in the bathroom. My head was spinning, and my face was stinging.

"Oh my God!" I screamed repeatedly.

I looked in the mirror and couldn't believe the sight I saw. I was enraged. I wasn't going to allow him to treat me like some regular chick. I was going to pack my bags and go back to my grandmother's house. Our marriage was fresh, so I could have it annulled. I was furious and wanted to take his head off. However, my spinning head said to be easy. I ran the bath water and took off my clothing. I couldn't figure out for the life of me what happened to the sweet and gentle man that I had married. I was upset with myself for allowing myself to get into yet another domestic violence situation. I knew my grandmother was having a fit up in heaven. I shook my head in disappointment. As I slid into the tub, I let the tears fall in the water. I was truly devastated. I made the worst decisions in my life with regards to a man. I sighed as I submerged my body into the water.

"Baby," Quincy lightly called out to me as he tapped on the bathroom door.

I closed my eyes and hoped that he would go away if I ignored him. It didn't work, for he began to bang louder. Not wanting to upset him anymore than he already was, I answered.

"Yes." I was slightly annoyed.

I wanted to bathe in peace and call it a night. I was so ready to get back home and return to my life. What I thought was a dream come true turned out to be my worst nightmare.

"I'm sorry, baby. Please let me in," he pleaded with me.

His begging was sickening. I was truly disgusted at how he could put his hands on me and then beg for my forgiveness.

"Bastard," I mumbled under my breath.

He banged on the door louder. "Janell!"

"The door is open," I yelled back at him.

I didn't want to hear him screaming anymore. My head was pounding, and I just wanted to go home. He entered the bathroom with his head hanging down. He approached the bathtub and kneeled down to my face. I acted as if he wasn't there. He sighed and touched my face. I shuddered and shrank back away from him.

"I don't want you to be afraid of me. I am so sorry for what happened just now. I don't know what got into me," he whispered to me.

"I don't care anything about your personal problems, 'because they aren't mines to bear. I want a divorce. This is not gonna work out," I confidently spat at him; I was so serious.

"So just like that, you wanna leave me? You got it twisted, little mama." He laughed. "This right here is 'til death do us part. So, you can try to leave all you want," he threatened.

I couldn't believe what I was hearing. *Not again*! I screamed in my head as he walked out of the bathroom, laughing at me.

When Quincy and I got back to New York, things took a turn for the worse. The abuse got worse and worse. This time I had to hide black eyes and busted noses. I hated makeup but learned to apply it to my bruised face. He isolated me from my friends. My number was changed and so was my zip code. He moved me from the hood to SoHo, a nice neighborhood in lower Manhattan. Famous for its trendy boutiques and restaurants, there were always crowds of people around. I wasn't used to living among white faces. It was a huge adjustment for me. My husband was an investment banker who worked in a Fortune 500 company. So not only did I have to live among white people, I had to socialize with them at company parties. I'm not racist, it was just something about being the only black person among a group of white people that made me nervous.

Days turned into weeks and weeks turned into months. I was extremely worn and battered. Every damn day there was a problem in my house. I couldn't take anymore. I was extremely depressed and feeling suicidal; I had nothing to live for. Everything that I loved in life he took from me. I couldn't be around Venessa, I couldn't wear what I wanted to wear, and I had to wear makeup every day. I was miserable and longing for a way out of this bull.

## Chapter Ten

On occasion, my husband let me go out. I took that opportunity to go see Venessa. She lived in my old apartment. My nerves were shot as I traveled uptown to my old neighborhood. I was going crazy and didn't know what to do with myself. My life was slowly crumbling right in front of me.

I thought that I would be having a relaxing day with my best friend, but it didn't turn out that way. I ended up being rushed to the emergency room for severe dehydration and on top of that, discovering that I was pregnant. Being that I was unconscious when I was picked up, all of my bruises and scars were exposed. When I woke up, I had a very sad-looking Venessa staring down at me.

"Why you are looking at me like that?" I whispered. My throat was on fire. My arms were sore.

"Why didn't you tell me he was beating you? You're not a punching bag!" she screamed.

I didn't say anything, because I didn't know what to say. She was right.

There was a knock at the door and two police detectives entered. They asked me all kinds of disturbing and painful questions. "Is your husband abusing you? How long has it been going on?" I knew my answers would get my husband arrested, but at this point, I didn't care. I had someone inside of me that I needed to protect from their father. I rubbed my belly and prayed for this whole ordeal to be over.

When I was released from the hospital, I moved back into my old apartment. Venessa had some guy friends of hers go to get my stuff from the home I had shared with Quincy. I wasn't feeling comfortable at all; fear was consuming me. I knew my husband had gotten wind of what I had done to him. I knew he was going to come looking for me; I knew my life was in danger. Everyone around me swore that everything would be okay, but I begged to differ.

To help relax my mind, Venessa had set up a birthday party for me. I didn't care about turning twenty-five. I was pregnant, married to a psycho, and severely depressed. However, to make my friend happy, I let her do what she wanted to help me celebrate my day. I had one thing on my mind and that was my upcoming doctor's appointment. I was eighteen weeks and going to find out the sex of my baby, a baby that I shared with an evil man. I didn't know how something so beautiful, could come out of something so ugly. I was disappointed in myself for the poor decisions I had made and kept making. From this moment on, I made a promise to stop making stupid decisions.

My twenty-fifth birthday was lit! Venessa really did her thing. She rented out a house in upstate New York and had a bunch of our friends come up. I didn't know any of the men. I wasn't trying to, but this one particular one wouldn't stop staring at me. Chauncey was a cutie, but I wasn't interested. I had more than enough problems in my life at the time, and definitely didn't need another. I ended up spending a huge chunk of time with him and I truly enjoyed myself. My mind however was on someone else. A blast from my past that called me to wish me a happy birthday.

They say absence makes the heart grow fonder; I totally agree. I was truly hurt when Dwayne and I broke up. We split, because at the time, he and I wanted different things out of life. When he was with me, he was with four other girls. I knew that and didn't care at the time. After a while, it started getting to me, so I removed myself from the situation.

When Dwayne got back in touch with me, I was ecstatic. I missed him after all these years. He was like a breath of fresh air to my toxic, unpleasant marriage. It was hard to sneak around my husband, but I managed to meet up with Dwayne several times. Dwayne was the one who gave me the strength and courage to leave my husband. It was so crazy; my daughter should have given me the strength to leave. I love my daughter, but at the time, I saw her as a pawn in my husband's

evil game. He said I could leave, but I had to
leave her behind. He placed me in a catch-22
position. If I left, I would never see my child
again and if I stayed, I would have to endure
hell for the rest of my life. As the days went on,
I became so weary. The only good thing in my
life was the fact that I had graduated from
community college with a paralegal certificate
and was now enrolled in a university for a
political science degree. School was my one
and only solace, the place I could run to escape
all of my pain and sorrows.


I nearly fainted when I was told
the news; I was having a girl. I turned away
from the screen. *A little girl*? How was I to
protect her when I couldn't even protect
myself from the man that I was married to? It
was definitely about to get real. Quincy and I

met up a few times; he begged me to come home. He was highly upset that he had to spend the night in jail and pay $20,000 bail. I didn't care; I just want wanted him to know he had a child coming. He was ecstatic and wanted us to be a family again. I told him that was definitely not going to happen. I told him that I wanted a divorce; I wanted my life and everything that he stole from me back. As I walked away, I knew I was in for the fight of my life.

## Chapter Eleven

I went back home with my husband. It just made more sense to be with him instead of live in fear of not knowing what he would do to me. At least in the house, I knew what to expect; the streets, not so much. I thought things would get better, because I was pregnant with a little girl. For the remainder of my pregnancy, he was a gentleman. I was shocked and had to pinch myself a few times to make sure I was awake. I was living in such a fantasy world while I was pregnant that I didn't prepare myself for what was to come once I gave birth.

Katrina Dior Richardson was born at three a.m. on a Monday morning. I was in the most hurtful pain, and my dear husband ignored me while I cried out in agony. While I was lying down, I felt a gush of water come out of me. Quincy must have felt it too, because he jumped out the bed. I just laid there and screamed. It was then that he moved his slow ass and took me to the hospital. By the time we got there, I didn't have time to get any drugs or any type of relief. I delivered an eight-pound baby, naturally. That nearly tore me apart, literally. I swore I didn't want any more kids after her. This was my first baby and my husband expected me to know what to do all the time. I was exhausted and he was constantly yelling and complaining. I was just waiting for something to give. I had had enough but needed a reason to just walk away.

The day that bastard husband of mine brought a female home to live with us, was the day I said enough is enough. I knew she was trying to be like me, because I saw she was rocking my outfits right out of my closet! Quincy even spent most of his time at home with her. Which was fine, because he and I were done; at least in my head. With Melinda around, I got some of my freedom back. I was so glad and wanted to kiss her to thank her, but I wasn't a lesbian, so I just took whatever freedom was afforded to me and did what I wanted to do. Doing what I wanted to do almost cost me my life.

*********************************************

One of the most important things in life are boundaries I wasn't taught boundaries. I had no idea that I taught people how to treat me. I also didn't know that I didn't have to just accept whatever ugly behavior people displayed to me. Because I had no boundaries in place in my marriage, I allowed my husband to disrespect me time and time again. It got so bad that he nearly killed me during a scuffle. The day that I attempted to leave he wasn't haven it. He had a gun pointed at my head. I grew angry and started hitting him. The gun went off knocking me to the ground. I heard another shot and then everything went black.

■■■■■■■■■■■■■■■■■■■■■■■■■■■■■■■■■■■■■■■■■

My dear beloved husband took his life and tried to take mine. I couldn't believe that I was lying in a puddle of my own blood. However, that's what I get for being so stupid. Men were and would always be my weakness. I know my grandmother is looking down on me and shaking her head. I hated that I was disappointing her.

I attempted to clean up my life. In doing so, I cut off all toxic and negative people in my life. As I did this, I noticed positive things started happening. I was at a peaceful place in my life. I was grateful to Dwayne for helping me escape my nightmare, but I had to cut him

loose as well. I thought he was Mr. Nice Guy
when in fact; he had a wife and a son. Men
were just ridiculous to me. None of them could
tell the truth. Not even the one I was currently
dating. Chauncey is that dude. He has the
swag and sex appeal I desired out of my man,
but he was different in a way. He was very
family-oriented, which is funny, because he
lied about having kids in the first place.
Nevertheless, I understood why he did it. Hell,
I wouldn't even have talked to him, knowing
he had two kids and two moms. I never
wanted to be a part of a situation like his, yet,
here I was.

We'd just started dating for the past six
months, but we had been talking ever since the
birthday party. I didn't get as close to him as I
usually did with other men. I felt that if I got
close to him, things would go wrong like they
did in my other relationships. Sadly, Chauncey

was paying for the mistake's men made in my life. I had a wall up and I wanted to see if he was going to try to climb it before I gave my heart to him. I know you probably are confused on what I just explained. You're not the only one. I decided after the death of my husband to be with Dwayne.

Dwayne was a good friend to me. I know him for a long time. He was there throughout the whole Quincy ordeal. I thought I knew him but surprise I did not. I find out that he had a wife and child. I was so done with him! With all the drama and chaos, I turned to Chauncey. I know I shouldn't have but he turned out to be a good friend. This time I wanted to take my time and do everything right. I was so sick of getting my heart broken. Falling in love after getting hurt so many times just doesn't feel right. But I want to try to love this man that is loving all over me and my daughter.

## Chapter Twelve

There is a light at the end of the tunnel. Sounds so cliché but it's true. I have been through hell and back. Almost lost my life twice. Had my spirit broken by my mother and men that I trusted and loved. And yet I am still here. I am still here to tell the story of abuse, hurt and pain I went through. You can survive anything you are going thorough. You have to want to. You have to change the narrative and stop blaming others for the things that happen to you. Yes, they cause us pain, but we cause our own pain by staying in places we don't belong. Healing is a process and however long it takes I am going to go for the ride.

I am very happy to say I graduated and am on my way to law school. I was so determined to make my grandmother proud. I strived to be the best student I could even with all the madness going on in my life. The man that I now love and adore had a lot to do with it. After two domestic violence incidents and scars all over my body, I felt ugly and broken. I didn't understand what he saw in me. I had to learn to love myself all over again. He gave me the space and time to do that. He stayed around when I yelled, cried, and rejected him. He stayed around when I felt like crap, felt lower than the ground and didn't want to continue with life. He gave me the encouragement, love and care that I needed.

I constantly asked God "Why is he here?" I honestly believe he was sent by my

Grandma to look after me and be my support system. No one can ever replace my Grandma. I just appreciate everything that he does for me our children.

Despite my childhood, I managed to make something out of myself. It wasn't easy pulling myself up off the ground most days, but I did it with the support of my man and people I call family. I don't know where I would be without them. I really am in peaceful place and can't wait for what's next in my life.

The most important thing I had to learn in my healing process is how to forgive. How do we forgive the people who hurt us the most? Do we forgive and forget? Does forgiving them excuse their behavior. The answer to both questions is no. We forgive with no expectations for our personal peace. We are human so forgetting is kind of hard to do. I know that I will never forget the heartache and pain that I have experienced. I feel that it has shaped me and made me into the person who I am today.

The people who hurt me have to answer for what they have done. That is none of my concern where and when. I did my part to bring me peace. Some people the forgiveness process was simple and others it was difficult, and I didn't get the closure that I felt I deserved. My father and I have started to develop a relationship. It's a struggle because I don't know him, and he doesn't know me. It feels weird, I guess. But since he's willing, I'm willing to make things work.

As far as Dwayne and my mom go, they don't want to acknowledge their actions. Having a conversation was very difficult because I was always wrong or told they didn't say or do what I said they did. I just couldn't deal with it and left it alone. I forgive them and am moving on with my life.

Life is strange. Where one comes from does not indicate where they are going. I can make the choice to be better than my situation or just accept it. I don't want to accept anything than the best in life. I have so much to look forward to and I refuse to let my past hold me back. To persevere means to keep moving in the midst of adversity. I could have easily broken down and quit school when my grandma died. But I didn't. I want and need more out of life than what I currently have. My spirit was broken so many times, but I decided to keep on moving. We all have choices to make. I choose to be the best version of myself every day.

The End

Sheri Simmons & Shavona Warmington

# Message from Sheri

Thank you for reading my short story in this anthology. Some parts of this story are true. I am a domestic violence survivor. If there are any survivors or people currently in this situation, please get help. I know firsthand that it is not easy. There are resources available!

I can be reached at

FromPaintoPurposeInc@gmail.com

Instagram @frompaintopurposellc

Facebook Page- From Pain to Purpose


Check out my other books

Nicole's Story

Divine Assignment

My Financial Story: What Not to Do with Money

Autographed Copies can be purchased from my website, Consultwithsheri.com

*The Power of Perseverance*

*Coming Soon*

You Know My Name, Not My Story (My Memoir)

Divine Assignment Book 2

Healing Begins with You Journal

**Thank you again**

**Sheri N. Simmons**